C0-DVV-716

FRANCISCAN MONTESSORI
EARTH SCHOOL
LIBRARY

CLIMATE CHANGE

MYTHS AND CONTROVERSIES

BY JIM OLLHOFF

FRANCISCAN MONTESSORI
EARTH SCHOOL
LIBRARY

VISIT US AT
WWW.ABDOPUBLISHING.COM

Published by ABDO Publishing Company, 8000 West 78th Street, Suite 310, Edina, MN 55439. Copyright ©2011 by Abdo Consulting Group, Inc. International copyrights reserved in all countries. No part of this book may be reproduced in any form without written permission from the publisher. ABDO & Daughters™ is a trademark and logo of ABDO Publishing Company.

Printed in the United States of America, North Mankato, Minnesota
052010
092010

 PRINTED ON RECYCLED PAPER

Editor: John Hamilton
Graphic Design: Sue Hamilton
Cover Photos: iStockphoto
Interior Photo: AP-pgs 5, 9, 13, 19, 21, 22, 23 & 26; Dion Manastyrski-Ministry of Forest-pg 28; Getty Images-pgs 10, 11, 17 & 18; Glacier National Park-pg 8; iStockphoto-pgs 1, 4, 6, 7 9, 25, 28 & 32; NASA-pg 16; Thinkstock-pgs 14, 15 & 29; *Time* Magazine-pg 24.

Library of Congress Cataloging-in-Publication Data

Ollhoff, Jim, 1959-
   Myths and controversies / Jim Ollhoff.
       p. cm. - (Climate change)
   Includes index.
   ISBN 978-1-61613-454-9
   1. Global warming--Juvenile literature. 2. Climatic changes--Juvenile literature. I. Title.
   QC981.8.G56O56 2011
   363.738'74--dc22
                          2010005021

CONTENTS

INTRODUCTION

Why are there so many different opinions about climate change? Some people think climate change is a hoax. They think it is a giant conspiracy cooked up by scientists who want money from the government. Some people honestly try to understand climate change, but the science is sometimes too hard, so they give up. Some people have heard so many things that they don't know who or what to believe.

Climate change is on TV, in the newspapers, and on the Internet. There are raging debates about whether or not global warming is real. But among climate scientists, there is very little debate. The literature that scientists read, which is written by other scientists, largely points to one conclusion: the world's climate is warming, and human activity is to blame.

Many falsehoods, or myths, have been spread about climate change. Some of these myths have a kernel of truth in them. Some have been repeated so often that people think they are completely true. In the following pages, we'll identify some of the most common myths about global warming, along with what the scientific evidence really says.

Below: Climate change headlines are seen a lot today.

destruction of rain forests

climate pact

Extreme weather 'proves effect of global warming'

Climate change

Climate Change

Revival of nuclear plants

raising worries over waste

debate on global warming

coal-fired power plant

Above: A cyclist rides past a climate mosaic outside the United Nations Climate Change Conference in Montreal, Canada, in December 2005. Many falsehoods, or myths, have been spread about climate change. It is important to get the facts.

MYTH: THE WORLD WILL BECOME A GIANT FIREBALL

Facing Page: Even with global warming, the earth will not start on fire. *Below:* A changing climate will cause new rainfall patterns.

The earth will not melt, start on fire, or burn to ashes. Even with global warming, the earth itself will survive just fine. The human race will not go extinct. However, life will be much different than it is today. The more the earth warms, the more things will change.

A changing climate causes new rainfall patterns. Vegetation and farming practices will be different. Many animal species may become extinct when their habitats are destroyed. Insects may spread disease to more parts of the world. Glaciers may melt, leaving millions of people without drinking water. Low-lying areas of the world may flood, leaving millions of people homeless and causing mass migrations to higher ground.

People sometimes talk about "saving the earth." But actually, the earth doesn't need saving. It's our way of life that needs saving.

MYTH: A COLD DAY PROVES GLOBAL WARMING IS FALSE

Below: A 1914 photo of Glacier National Park's Blackfoot and Jackson glaciers shows the two connected. A 2009 photo shows how each glacier has melted and receded.

Have you ever looked out the window on a cold winter day and wondered, "Whatever happened to global warming?" You have to remember that there is a big difference between weather and climate. Weather is what's happening outside today or tomorrow. It happens in one place, at one time. There always has been, and always will be, a lot of changes in the weather from day to day, and from month to month.

Climate is what happens all over the earth, over many decades or centuries. Climate looks at the weather from all over the world, and records it over the long term. If the temperature goes up a few degrees in one place on a single day or week (weather), people who live there can put on a short-sleeve shirt until the thermometer comes back down to normal. But if the temperature goes up several degrees worldwide, for months or years, that results in droughts, floods, melting glaciers, heat waves, hurricanes, storms, and major upheaval.

Global warming does not mean that every single place on the earth will get warmer. Some places will indeed get warmer. Some will get scorchingly hot. But other places will get colder because changing conditions will pull Arctic air down to different areas. Some places will have more storms. Others will have more droughts. For this reason, many scientists prefer the term "climate change" instead of global warming, because not every place on the globe will warm. The earth is a very complex place, and changing its average temperature even a few degrees will have far-reaching effects.

Left and *Below:* In Nevada, Lake Mead's water levels have dropped more than 100 feet (30 m) in 10 years, causing serious concerns for the area. Lake Mead is both a recreational spot, as well as a provider of water to Las Vegas and the surrounding area.

MYTH: THE EARTH ISN'T REALLY WARMING

In the twentieth century, scientists first claimed that the earth was warming and human activity was to blame. Many people didn't believe them.

But as time went on, scientists were able to more accurately measure temperatures and the amount of carbon dioxide and other greenhouse gasses in the atmosphere. A disturbing picture began to emerge. Record heat waves struck in the late 1990s. There were increases in storms, and glaciers began rapidly melting.

Right: People stop for ice cream during a brutal New York City heat wave in 2006. The past two decades have seen record heat waves throughout the world.

Despite this evidence, a few people insist that the world is not warming. There are even some scientists among the doubters, but they are only a small fraction of the scientific community. The doubters say that because there have been no scorching heat waves like in the late 1990s, that the world is not warming. However, it is important to look at the larger picture, not just a year here and there.

Above: A girl cools off under a mister on a street in Palm Springs, California, in 2007. During the heat wave, temperatures reached 115 degrees Fahrenheit (46 degrees C).

Some people who say the world isn't warming give evidence of a few glaciers that are getting bigger—not melting. Some can be found in South America, the United States, and the Himalayan Mountains. Some people point to a stable ice sheet on one side of Antarctica. They claim it is proof that the earth isn't warming.

Indeed, there are a few glaciers in the world that are getting bigger. However, most glaciers across the world are melting and getting smaller. It's not a good argument to say that one growing glacier means that the earth isn't warming. It's a little like saying that since a turkey is a bird, and turkeys can't fly, then no birds can fly.

In Antarctica, there is an ice sheet on the eastern side of the continent that has been stable. This stability was likely caused by a hole in the ozone layer in the atmosphere. The ozone hole changed the weather, causing colder air to blow more quickly across the east side of the continent. However, measurements in 2002 and later found that even the east side of Antarctica is now losing ice.

When scientists analyze all the measurements from satellites, weather stations, and tracking centers around the world, the evidence is clear: the world's climate is getting warmer. Studies show that the climate has already warmed almost 1 degree Celsius (about 1.8 degrees Fahrenheit) over the past century.

Facing Page: While global warming is causing the retreat of glaciers in the Sierra Nevadas, Cascades, and Rocky Mountains, the Hotlum glacier on the northeast face of California's Mt. Shasta is growing.

12

MYTH: WARMING IS JUST A NATURAL PROCESS

Below: Molten lava explodes from a volcano in Hawaii. There hasn't been enough volcanic activity in the last century to cause today's global warming.

Some people agree that the earth is warming, but say it's not because of human activity. They say that warming is just a natural process, that the earth always warms and cools, and it is currently in a natural warming stage. There are some geologists who say that the world is warming because of volcanoes. Some people say that increased sun activity is causing the heat.

The world is a very complex place, with many things contributing to heat buildup. The problem with some of the "natural" explanations is that there isn't enough evidence to support them. There hasn't been enough volcanic activity in the last century to cause such a drastic heat increase, and the sun's activity hasn't been any more intense than usual.

The earth does indeed have natural cooling and warming periods. However, the warming seen in the past 150 years has been significantly more than any warming period ever recorded. It started during the days of the Industrial Revolution. Since then, humans have been putting more and more carbon dioxide in the air through the burning of fossil fuels. And carbon dioxide is one thing scientists know for sure causes warming.

Above: A coal-fired power plant spews carbon dioxide into the air. Scientists know for sure that burning fossil fuels does cause global warming.

MYTH: WE'LL BE BETTER OFF WHEN IT'S WARMER

Below: A map shows how Arctic sea ice has receded in the Northwest Passage.

SEA ICE CONCENTRATION (PERCENT)

0   50   100

People who believe this myth usually give three examples: the Northwest Passage, oil in the Arctic, and how plants consume carbon dioxide.

The first example is the Northwest Passage. This is a shipping route in the Arctic waters north of Canada. In the past, it has been covered by ice most or all of the year. In a warmer world, this water will be ice-free much of the year. Therefore, ships going from the Atlantic Ocean to the Pacific Ocean will have a shorter route than going through the Panama Canal. So, it's true that the few people who own ships that have to make that journey will save money. But for everyone else, warming will cause severe problems.

Ice breaks up along the Northwest Passage in the spring.

The second example focuses on Arctic resources. Geologists believe there are large quantities of oil beneath the ice that covers the region around the earth's North Pole. When the Arctic is ice-free, those resources will be available for drilling. Many countries and companies are already trying to take or buy land in the Arctic region. The problem, of course, is that drilling for oil will eventually mean the burning of even more fossil fuels. And the burning of fossil fuels is what changed the climate in the first place.

Below: An oil platform in Alaska. If the Arctic becomes ice-free, large quantities of oil will be available for drilling.

People sometimes give a third example of why things will be better in a warmer climate. They say that since plants consume carbon dioxide, the earth will be better for plants. They say that the more carbon dioxide that is in the air, the more vegetation and crops will grow. But there are several problems with this view. There is no evidence that increased vegetation will be widespread. In fact, some studies suggest that more carbon dioxide is not necessarily good for plants. Beyond a certain level, plants simply shut down, and don't convert any more carbon dioxide into oxygen. Further, while it's possible that forests may get a boost from the extra carbon dioxide, this idea doesn't consider problems caused by increased forest fires and insect invaders.

The biggest problem with this myth is that it doesn't take into account the other side of the equation. What about the millions of people who live in low-lying areas of Bangladesh or India, which are areas that will be underwater? Will they be better off? What about the tens of thousands of people in the western United States who will face chronic water shortages? What about the billions of dollars it will cost to build levees to keep rising waters out of Florida or New Orleans, Louisiana?

Above: People wade through floodwaters in India in October 2009. Hundreds of people died and thousands lost their homes due to flooding that year.

MYTH: SCIENTISTS ARE STILL ARGUING ABOUT CLIMATE CHANGE

Facing page:
Former United States Vice President Al Gore works to promote understanding about climate change, and what can be done to stop global warming.

This is a myth that many people believe. Much of the misinformation claims that scientists are still arguing about climate change, and that only a few scientists really believe it. One Internet rumor claims that 50,000 scientists have signed a petition saying they don't agree with global warming. This isn't true.

More than 95 percent of climate scientists believe the evidence of global warming. They see the effects of climate change every day. Scientists who aren't experts about the climate, such as geologists, may not all agree that global warming is a big problem. But the more people know about climate science, the more likely they are to see and understand the issues of global warming.

In 1988, the United Nations started an organization called the Intergovernmental Panel on Climate Change (IPCC). This group's job is to read and analyze climate change research studies from all over the world, and then advise governments. They published lengthy reports in 1990, 1992, 1995, 2001, and 2007. The IPCC is made up of scientists from 130 different countries. They make use of more than 2,500 scientists who review research, and more than 800 scientists who help write the reports.

Below: Rajendra Pachauri has been head of the IPCC since 2002. The IPCC's job is to read and analyze climate change research studies from all over the world, and then advise governments.

The IPCC said in its 2007 report, "Warming of the climate system is unequivocal." This means that there is no question that the climate is warming. For the vast majority of scientists, there is no longer any debate that the world is warming.

Scientists are also no longer debating whether humans are responsible—they have already reached that conclusion. Today, scientists debate not the existence or the causes of global warming, but the effects it will have, how fast it will happen, and what we can do to stop it.

Rajendra Pachauri
Chairman IPCC

Above: Rajendra Pachauri, of India, chair of the Intergovernmental Panel on Climate Change, former British Prime Minister Tony Blair, California Governor Arnold Schwarzenegger, and moderator Anne Thompson, Chief Environmental Affairs correspondent for NBC News, participate in a climate control discussion at the second Governors' Global Climate Summit in Los Angeles, California, in 2009.

MYTH: SCIENTISTS PREDICTED GLOBAL COOLING IN THE 1970s

Above: In the 1970s, a handful of scientists predicted global cooling. Since that time, thousands of articles have been written about global warming.

In the 1970s, a handful of scientists predicted global cooling. That was in reaction to a highly toxic pollutant called sulfur dioxide, a chemical that causes rain to become acidic. A few scientists said that if this pollutant wasn't reduced, the earth's climate might cool. In the 1980s, industry greatly reduced its use of sulfur dioxide.

In the entire decade of the 1970s, only seven scientific papers were written warning that the earth might cool. In the last decade, thousands of scientific papers have been written about global warming.

Some people today believe that in the 1970s, most scientists feared global cooling. Since it didn't happen, why should we believe the scientists today who warn about global warming? But that's not true. In the 1970s, there was no such agreement among scientists. Only seven papers warned of global cooling. Today, there is a definite consensus, or agreement, among climate scientists that the earth is warming. The evidence is overwhelming.

Above: In the 1970s, global cooling was a topic that grew out of a concern regarding the highly toxic pollutant called sulfur dioxide.

WHAT SCIENTISTS REALLY DON'T KNOW

There are some things, of course, that scientists don't know. They don't know how much the earth will warm. That really depends on how fast we stop producing greenhouse gasses. If greenhouse gasses are reduced quickly, the earth may not warm very much at all. If we keep adding more and more gasses to the atmosphere, the climate will warm a lot.

Scientists don't know if global warming will start to make itself worse. In northern lands, such as Alaska and northern Canada, there is ground called permafrost. This is ground that is frozen most of the year. This permafrost has a lot of frozen vegetation in it. As the weather warms, the permafrost will thaw, releasing even more carbon dioxide and methane into the air. Will new plants, growing in the newly thawed soil, absorb all the extra carbon dioxide? Or will the released carbon and methane make global warming worse, like a runaway train? Scientists don't know the answer. However, they know that the permafrost is already beginning to melt.

Facing Page:
The village of Shaktoolik, Alaska, faces land erosion and increased flooding caused by melting permafrost and a rise in sea levels due to warming climate.

Scientists debate how much carbon dioxide the oceans can absorb. Some scientists say that if the carbon dioxide content of the atmosphere gets higher, ocean plant life will stop absorbing carbon dioxide altogether. Other scientists say that ocean plant life will be able to absorb more than we think.

It is hard to predict the continuing effects of global warming, and the "domino effect" it might have on other systems. For example, in Colorado, freezing temperatures kill tree-damaging insects every year. If global warming causes temperature to seldom sink below freezing, will the insects live all year round? Will they move to new places? Could they, for example, move into areas and destroy vegetation that bears need to survive? If so, will the bears then turn to something else for food? Trying to trace all the effects—and the effects of the effects—of global warming is very difficult. We may never know exactly what will happen until it is too late.

Below: The mountain pine beetle bores into pine trees, killing the tree and turning it a dark brown. Pine beetle populations increase during long, warm summers. High populations of pine beetles would be devastating to pine forests.

Scientists debate how much carbon dioxide the oceans can absorb. Some scientists believe that if the carbon dioxide content of the atmosphere gets higher, ocean plant life will stop absorbing carbon dioxide altogether.

GLOSSARY

CARBON DIOXIDE

Normally a gas, carbon dioxide is a chemical compound made of two oxygen atoms and one carbon atom. Its chemical symbol is CO_2. It is created by burning fossil fuels. It is the leading cause of the greenhouse effect and global warming.

CLIMATE CHANGE

The climate of the earth, which consists of the weather all over the world for decades or centuries, and how it is changing.

FOSSIL FUEL

Fuels that are created from the remains of ancient plants and animals that were buried and then subjected to millions of years of heat, pressure, and bacteria. Oil and coal are the most common fossil fuels burned to create electricity. Natural gas is also a fossil fuel. Burning fossil fuels releases carbon dioxide into the atmosphere, contributing to global warming.

GEOLOGIST

A scientist who studies rocks to develop an understanding of the earth's history.

GLACIER

An immense sheet of ice that moves over land, growing and shrinking as the climate changes. Glaciers carve and shape the land beneath them. Glaciers today are found in the polar regions, and in mountainous areas. They hold vast reserves of fresh water.

GREENHOUSE GAS

Any gas that is good at absorbing and retaining the sun's heat. Carbon dioxide, which is released into the atmosphere by the burning of fossil fuels, is a greenhouse gas. Greenhouse gasses contribute to a gradual warming of the earth, which is called the greenhouse effect.

HIMALAYAN MOUNTAINS

A mountain range extending about 1,500 miles (2,414 k) along the border between India and the Tibet region of China, and through Pakistan, Nepal, and Bhutan.

INDUSTRIAL REVOLUTION

A time in the 1800s and 1900s when huge scientific advances were made in machine technology. The world's economies started relying more on manufacturing instead of farming and manual labor.

IPCC (INTERGOVERNMENTAL PANEL ON CLIMATE CHANGE)

An organization set up by the United Nations. The IPCC's job is to advise governments on the issue of climate change.

METHANE

A gas that is created when organic materials decay.

OZONE LAYER

An upper layer of the atmosphere containing high levels of ozone. Ozone is a gas known to absorb the sun's damaging ultraviolet radiation.

PERMAFROST

Frozen ground in areas such as Alaska and northern Canada.

UNITED NATIONS

Formed in 1945, an organization of representatives from 192 nations with the mission of promoting peace, security, and economic development on a world-wide basis.

INDEX